Frank Waters

The Water Lily

An oriental fairy tale

Frank Waters

The Water Lily
An oriental fairy tale

ISBN/EAN: 9783337174187

Printed in Europe, USA, Canada, Australia, Japan

Cover: Foto ©Andreas Hilbeck / pixelio.de

More available books at **www.hansebooks.com**

THE WATER LILY:

AN ORIENTAL FAIRY TALE

BY

FRANK WATERS.

————

OTTAWA:
J. DURIE & SON.
———
1888.

TO

HIS EXCELLENCY

THE MOST HONOURABLE

THE MARQUIS OF LANSDOWNE, G.C.M.G.,

GOVERNOR–GENERAL OF CANADA,

THE HEIR OF A NAME

ILLUSTRIOUS IN LETTERS AND STATESMANSHIP,

THIS POEM

IS, BY KIND PERMISSION,

DEDICATED,

WITH DEEP GRATITUDE AND RESPECT,

BY

THE AUTHOR.

PREFACE.

As regards the subject-matter of the following poem, I can lay claim to no originality. The story is taken from a very remarkable book, entitled "Oriental Fairy Tales," which I read once in early childhood, but have never since had the good fortune to meet with. The work is one of those in which,—as in " Lalla Rookh,"—a number of detached tales are strung, gem-like, on the golden thread of a connecting narrative; the central figure in this latter being the Wandering Angel, whose various experiences give rise to the different tales. At least, this is my recollection of the plan.

At the time when I read the book, I was far too young to be consciously aware of its exquisite beauty and deep significance; nevertheless, even then it made a lasting impression on me, especially this most charming and pathetic tale of The Water Lily. And so, when, many years later, while the first flush of poetry was still upon me, I met the tale, detached, in a book of readings published by the Messrs. Routledge, it took, on that second perusal, a permanent place in heart and mind, and became, to me, one of those waking and persistent dreams which haunt us all under many forms. To one gifted with the power of poetic expression, such dreams are as immaterial beings craving embodiment at his hands; and I forthwith commenced a versified rendering of the story; for, though the original is simply perfect as far as it goes, it is yet but a mere sketch; and I longed to fill in bodily to my mind's eye the delicious outlines, the magic lights and shades, which it vaguely suggested rather than supplied. But the work died, almost as soon as conceived; want of leisure, and a thousand other obstacles, stood in my way; and it was not until eight years afterwards,—in the latter part of '83,—that the haunting idea took permanent embodiment and shape under the stress of a sudden and sustained inspiration. In extenuation of any faults which the reader may see reason to impute to it, I may plead that the poem was written piecemeal, from day to day, amid innumerable distractions, and finished in less than four weeks. I will add—what I have already implied— that, though the story itself is not mine as regards the general outline, all the *details* are strictly my own: the colouring and shading of the picture are almost entirely, or altogether, my handiwork. Thus, the conception of the scene amid which the events take place, the child's midnight dream, her brooding reverie as she sits gazing on the lily,—all these, and other such passages, are my filling in of the fundamental sketch.

I shall add only a very few words as to the significance of the poem. Even in its obvious and merely superficial aspect—regarded as *only* an Oriental fairy tale—the story is yet well worth reading, and cannot but charm and touch those human sympathies to which it is the distinctive task of poetry to appeal. But, for those who can look below the surface, there is a soul of inner meaning to this body of external beauty and grace. For the story hints to us, rather than broadly speaks—(and it is only so, I venture to think, that poetry should attempt to convey moral lessons, at least in its sustained efforts)—it hints to us, not only of the strength and wonder of a mother's love, conquering all death and change; but also of that strange perversity in our nature which ever goads us on to yearn for that which is forbidden us; of the veiled destruction which so often awaits us even as we lay our hand on the prohibited prize; of the vanity with which men or angels would oppose the rulings of the ineffable and all-wise Providence that sways through all; and of the solemn certainty—bitter or sweet, as we ourselves make it—that all is best as it stands ordered for us, and that, in overstepping the bounds marked out for us, it may be but to fall over the brink of some blossom-hidden despair.

Such, as it seems to me, are a few of the deeper meanings which this truly exquisite little story may be legitimately held to convey to those who have ears to hear withal. And, if my work should be adjudged to possess no other merit—which I shall yet venture to hope may not be the case—it will still be a great consolation to me to think that, in an age when the public mind is so flooded with all that is loose and vicious in literature, my little effort has been put forth as a feeble dam thrown adventurously out into the roaring torrent of evil—to abide or be swept away as it lodges on men's hearts, or misses them and its object together.

CORNWALL, Ontario,   FRANK WATERS.
 January 3rd, 1888.

THE WATER LILY.

AN ORIENTAL FAIRY TALE.

Purple shades of eve were falling
   Softly through the amber air :
Far, the blind muezzin, calling,
   Bade the Moslemin to prayer.
From the westward, sunset still
   Flung a glory, brightly glowing,
O'er the plains, where many a rill,
   From the misty uplands flowing,
Caught the last reflection lent
   By the flaming occident,
Breaking the refracted beams
To a thousand quivering gleams,
Sapphire, ruby, emerald, gold,
Rainbow-tinted manifold.
Every little blade of grass
   Showed against that shining sky :
Every streamlet in its glass

Caught the splendour from on high.
'Twas the final flush of day,
Lingering ere it passed away ;
Like the dying smile of love,
  Over pallid features driven,
Ere the spirit soar above,
  Flitting to its native heaven.
Half the sky was tender bright
  As that heaven's dawning ray;
Half was darkening into night,
  Like the soul-abandoned clay.

Farther eastward, where the meadows
Stretched into the deepening shadows,
Lay the city—tower and wall ;
Humble hut and princely hall ;
Rich bazaar, with glittering stall ;
Squalid lane, whose houses tall
Clipt the footway mean and small :
Luxury and poverty
Elbowing each other by.
Now the shades of evening swept
  Like an ocean to its foot :
Higher up the walls they crept,

Beating with their billows mute
On the mouldering battlement,
Time-decayed and weather-rent,
Where the grass began to wave
Tall and rank as over a grave,
And the moss spread dank and dull,
Like the mould upon a skull.
All below was wrapt in shade ;
But, above, the sunset played,
Gold and crimson blending, yet,
Over dome and minaret,
Topping many a stately mosque,
Crowning many a light kiosk.
And the blind muezzin, standing
High on his aërial landing,
Felt the flush upon his face,
  Felt the glow upon his lid ;
  Felt that Fate from him had hid
All the glory, all the grace,
Of the hour and of the place :
Felt, and swelled his voice sonorous,
Gliding in its cadenced chorus
Down the golden grades of air,
Like an angel down the stair
Of the pure empyrean

Bearing news of Paradise
To the sluggish ear of man,
  In such learning little wise,
  Recking little of the skies.

Round, in gentle undulation,
  Richly-teeming, green, and fair,
Stretched a scene, the incarnation
Of each young imagination
Which the wild and sweet narration
  Of the bride of Schariar
Wakes, while thought is fresh and free,.
In the soul of infancy.
Here, the genie might have haunted
  Yonder grottoes, moss·o'ergrown ;
Here, the peri might have chanted,
  Keeping time unto the tone
  Of the fountain, bubbling lone,
  Dripping o'er the marble stone ;
Here, Aladdin might have wandered
  'Neath a grander palace dome,—
Love-sick Ganem mused and pondered,.
  As in Love's most favoured home :
Yonder copses might have hid

Genial Haroun Alraschid,
Roving on adventurous quest,
With grave Mesrour at his hest.
'Twas the very fabled scene
   Of those tales so sweetly told :
Here might every act have been,
   Written on their leaves of gold.

Far around the utmost rim
   Of horizon, closing all,
Rose the summits dusk and dim
   Of the distant mountain-wall ;
Faint as half-forgotten dream,
   When the morning opes our eyes,
And we grope athwart the stream
      Of our waking thought, to find
   The ideal, dim surmise
   Of some shadowy paradise,
   Lost 'mid the intricacies
      Of our night-thoughts, vague and blind.
North and south their crescent trending,
   Clipt the lovely land around ;
Huge its mighty horns extending
   Formed that Eden's utmost bound.
Now the westward peaks were red

As the heaven overhead ;
While, retreating toward the east,
Still their rosy glow decreased,
Ever fainter, duskier, dimmer,
Dying in a silvery shimmer
Where the moon began to grow
   Through the deepening orient heaven ;
Yet so faint you scarce might know
If 'twere she began to show,
Or some wreathéd tress of snow
   On the mountain-summit riven ;
Or a dewy mist, perchance,
Dimming twilight's dreamy glance.

But—its gem of rarest sheen,
Choicest jewel of the scene,—
   Six long bow-shots from the town,
With a palmy grove between,
   Shielding off the sombre frown
Of the ramparts old and grey,
   Lay a spot you well might seek
Vainly, through a summer's day,
   Dimpling deep on nature's cheek.
'Twas a green, sequestered dell,
Where the shelving meadows fell

Softly from a gentle swell
To the margin of a pond
Crystal-clear as diamond
Gleaming in the middle ground,
Cool, and darkling, and profound,
Girt with rosy thickets round.
To the east, the uplands rally
   In a gentle rise ;
To the west, they leave the valley
   Open to the skies.
Up the banks, their circling curves.
Show the greenest grassy turves,
Where the feathery fern droops o'er,
   Fluttering its lace-like plumes,
(Broidered with the clinging spore),
In each zephyr trembling o'er,
   Making pleasant lights and glooms.
Here and there, the wild rose, trailing
   O'er some crag enmossèd, grew ;
And its luscious sweets, exhaling
To the air with fragrance failing,
   Mingled with the breath which drew.
   Tenderly the violet blue,
Peeping shyly from the shade
By the rocky buttress made.

Purple hyacinths nodded slowly,
   Where the grass grew long and lush ;
Poppies, drowsed with melancholy,
   Bloomed into that dark-red flush
Which the opium-eater shows,
When the sleepy nectar flows
Throbbingly through every vein,
With a joy akin to pain.
Crimsoned fox-glove hung its standard
   Down the warm and sunny slope ;
And the glossy vine meandered,
     Thick with globy clusters, round
     Shrub and stone ; and to the ground
   Clung its tendrils, fast as hope
Clingeth even to glaze-eyed death,
Parting but with parted breath.

Many a homely floral sweet
   Of our rugged northern clime
Decked that chosen beauty-seat ;
But it boasted richer sweet
   Of its own wild orient prime :
Starry blossoms such as blow
Never in our fields of snow,—
Glowing tinctures, sunbow-dyes,

Like the hues of paradise
Half-revealed through evening skies ;
Wondrous forms, devices rare,
Nature's mouldings, quaint and fair,—
Trumpet-blossoms, deep and large,
 For the merry Puck to blow ;
Moon-like discs for Oberon's targe ;
Petals fashioned like a barge,
 Such as might Titania row ;
Orchid bloom, like bees, that hive
 In themselves the honied sweet,
With the murmurous flies alive
  When the molten noonbeams beat
  Through the air the pulse of heat ;
Red geraniums, all aflame,
Scarlet as a maiden's shame,
With their burning fringes set
Round the taper minaret
Of the long receptacle,
Slender as a heron's bill ;
Rich leguminosæ there
Danced and hovered in the air,
Moth-like with their fourfold wings,
And their nimble flutterings :
For the very blossoms seemed

2

Here to blossom into life,
As if the lovely land o'erteemed
   The vital power with which 'twas rife,
Through every pore, in forms undreamed
   Otherwise, of joyous life.
And from every stalk-held cup—
   Turban-tulips, streaked with gold ;
Maiden lilies, lifting up
   Their silver chalice, chaste of mould ;
   Violets, roses, fold on fold,
To the atmosphere laid bare,
Till it swooned with sweetness there :—
From all there breathed a fragrance, such.
   As the heavenly censers yield,
   Which the choral angels wield,
   When they bend before their King,
   Adoring, and adoring sing.
And every odour, like a touch
From the hand of her you love,
Darted through the frame, and drove
Burning blood through every vein,
From the heart unto the brain,
From the head unto the feet ;
A lightning-footed current fleet,
Pulsing with a pleasant heat,

Like the lover's passion sweet,
Keeping time to each heart-beat.

Midway lay the lake asleep
  'Neath the tender sky ;
With its waters calm and deep
  Glassing heavens on high,
'Twas an oval, stilly pool,
Dark and mirror-like, and cool,
Ruffled but at either end,
Where its waters take and send
The tribute stream adown the slope,
Like a flying antelope :
A little stream, that eastward fell
Down the green and quiet dell,
From the uplands, cedar-crowned,
Wakening murmurous echoes round,
That from slope to slope rebound
With sweet and melancholy sound,
Babbling o'er the sunny shallows,
  Shrilling o'er the pebbles clear,
  Parting, darting, there and here,
    Tumbling o'er the mossy rock,
Making little rainbow halos
  Where the whirling eddies rock,

And the glancing bubbles swim
Many-coloured round the rim ;
So it leaped from shelf to shelf,
Nimble-footed as an elf ;
So it wound meandering down
 The verdant slopings of the vale,
Like a silver scarf outblown
 On the flutterings of the gale.
Now along the lower valley
Run its ripples musically,
 Like a hand o'er flashing keys ;
Many a whirling rout and rally,
Many a playful flight and sally
 Mark the green intricacies
 Of its course round rocks and trees.
Here it glides, as lulled to sleep,
Where the shade is dark and deep ;
There, anon, its ripples run,
Dancing, out into the sun,
Tumbling over one another
With a laughter naught can smother.
Many a circling sweep it made,
Half in light and half in shade,
Where the network canopy
 Of the foliage lightly woven,

Wavered like inconstancy
'Neath each zephyr blowing free,—
 Meeting, parting, knit, and cloven ;
Nature's own kaleidoscope,
Changeful as a lover's hope :
And every lightest change above
 Was mirrored in the stream below,
As Beauty in the soul of Love,
 Where her every mood doth show :
Pleasant were those flecks of light,
 Pleasant were those shadows green,
  Dancing on the rivulet,
  Glancing on the blossoms wet
With the spray-drops large and bright,
 Quivering with liquid sheen.
But, oh ! most pleasant were the groves
 Of sweet musk-roses blowing round,
And peopled by the turtle doves,
Where a thousand cooing loves
 All day long kept swooning sound,
Half asleep and half awake,
Round the borders of the lake.
And *very* pleasant was the gush
 Of the waters clear and cool,
Where through flowering sedge and rush,

With a bubble, foam, and gush,
   They fell into the outer pool :
Yea ! sweet, within that sultry clime,
Their plashing fall, their silvery chime,
Their murmuring music, low and mellow,
Where they evoke a mimic billow
'Neath the branches of the willow,
Whose hoary trunk and silvern sheen
   Of weeping foliage, slantwise hung
Across that archway's darker green
Spanning the streamlet's course within,
   And o'er the wave its shadow flung—
The only sadness brooding there :
One cloud upon the summer air ;
One tear amid a thousand smiles ;
One thorn amid Hesperian isles.

But the lakelet was most fair :
   Every little blade of grass,
Every blossom blowing there,
Every tint and cloud of air,
   Lent a beauty to its glass :
Every leaf upon the tree
There was mirrored faithfully :
Every tree grew branching there

Through a yet more limpid air :
All the winding shores around
Doubled every slope and mound
Edged and rounded in the clear
Of the sunshine and the mere :
Every palmy promontory,
   Every stretch of pebbly beach,
Took therein a softer glory,
   Stretching downward, seemed to reach
Into realms more lovely yet
Than the scene in which 'twas set—
Fairy regions, sloping down
Into crystal deeps unknown,
Where the feathery clouds were strewn
As low along the nether sky
As their fellows floated high.
And so clear the waters were—
Lucent as a denser air,
Scarce you might perceive them there :
More it seemed as through a rent
In the sphere your glance were sent
To the under firmament.
'Twas like standing by a void,
   Looking clear from sky to sky,
   Heaven beneath and heaven on high,

And, between them poised and buoyed,
The sunny shore, its flowers and trees,
Floating o'er aërial seas.

Dost thou deem that I have lingered
　　Too minutely o'er the scene?
Else my theme were poorly fingered,
Had I not so dwelt and lingered :—
　　Nature is the go-between
Of a loving earth and heaven—
Unto her the sign is given,
And by her the token rendered :
And her service here is tendered,
That thy mind, attuned by her
To a mood the holier,
May through her be given to see
Part of that wide Mystery
Of which she holds the master-key—
The Underneath, Around, Above,
The Heart of Man, the Heart of Love !
*　*　*　*　*　*　*　*
Who sits upon the sloping marge,
　　Beside the glassy pool?
Who looks upon the lily-barge,
　　Nigh floating in the cool?

O little child, who dreamest there,
The evening glory on thy hair,
The deepening twilight in thine eyes,
The far-off splendour of its skies,—
Or art thou, truly, of the earth?
  Or from the evening star,
Just throeing to its silvery birth,
A beam embodied, hast come forth,
  Down-floating from afar?
For such thy dreamy beauties are,—
Thy loveliness is similar.

She sits upon the sloping marge,
  She gazes on the pool,
She looks upon the lily-barge
  Nigh floating in the cool:
She bends above the shining glass;
  She stretches out her little hand;
She holdeth by the tufted grass,
  And by the wild vine's trailing strand:
She strives to grasp the shining bowl
On which the longing of her soul
Hath settled like the dragon-fly,
  Whose slender azure body shows
As might one blue vein wandering by
  Upon a maiden's brow of snows.

She wooes it nearer still to glide ;
  And just her rosy finger-tips
Can touch its gently curving side ;
  But, on the touch, adown it dips,
And o'er the limpid wave doth slide ;
  As, riding at their anchor, ships
Swing slowly round, in circlings wide,
Upon the drifting of the tide.
And then she smiles, and then she sighs,
And, bending out, again she tries,
The light of longing in her eyes ;
And once again it slowly flies,
And circles out, a fairy boat,
'Mid the large leaves that round it float ;
Just sailing on so lazily
That not the drowsy dragon-fly
Moves from his perch, nor stirs a wing
Into one moment's quivering.

O little child, so sweet and fair,
The evening glory on thy hair,
Thou doest wrong to linger there.
Was't not last eve thy mother spake ?
" My child ! my star ! avoid the lake !
For though it looks so warm and bright,

And though its deeps reflect the light,
Within it dwells a wicked sprite :
An evil genie lurks beneath ;
And he would suck away thy breath :
My child ! my star ! beware of Death ! ''

And in the night, when, in thy bed,
The pillow swelled around thy head,
And from the drowsy coverlet,
With poppy-dews of slumber wet,
The prickly sleep crept through and through
Thy form relaxed, as summer dew
Drenches a moonbeam folded flower,—
   Didst thou not seem in sleep to see
The lilied lake, the Evil Power
   That lurked beneath, to capture thee ?
Far, in that dim and swooning dream,
   The moonlight shimmered o'er the lake ;
And nothing save the murmuring stream,
   And the low wind, and thou, did wake.
Above the brook, the arch of trees
   Yawned darkly, like a dragon's throat,
Wherein engulphed, the moaning breeze
   Died out in mutterings far remote.
The hoary willow glinted gray

Athwart the dark and hollow chasm,.
And slowly stirred its waving spray,
　　There hanging like a white miasm ;
While, down below, the shrivelled trunk
Showed like a grisly, cowlèd monk,
With skinny arms uplift to curse
The moon, the stars, the universe.
From bank to bank, the waveless mere
　　Was oily-black with shade,
Save where the moonbeams cold and clear
　　A ghostly glimmer made :
And over every lily's cup
　　There hung a vapour dense and dank,
From the black water steaming up—
　　A poisonous mist, that rose and sank,
And, ever and anon, would ape
Some weird, uncouth, half-human shape,
That seemed to gibber, mow, and cower,.
With elvish malice, in the flower.
And on thy soul there fell a fear,
　　And o'er thy heart it hung ;
Like the dim vapours of the mere,
　　It touched, and grew, and clung.
For now thy glances seemed to sink
Below the faintly-glinting brink,

And clomb adown the dusky grades
Of liquid deeps and sullen shades.
And now, the huge and bloated stems
  Of lilies, and those mighty weeds
  The slimy ooze prolific breeds,
Stretched up, like giant reptile limbs,
Or vast antennæ reaching out,
And groping in the gloom about;
Or, like those fabled monstrous snakes
That swell and puff in poisonous lakes,
Their thick and fleshy windings grew,
With unctuous gleam, the darkness through,
Or, darker shadows, seemed to wind
Around the fainter gloom behind.
And o'er thy trance the chilly fear
  More dense and heavy hung—
Like the white vapours of the mere,
  It touched, and grew, and clung.
For now, amid those monstrous shoots
That writhed up from pulpy roots—
White, clammy tubes, like veins by force
Plucked from a cold and rotting corse—
There grew a Presence dread and dim,
  A shade in shade, a deep in deep,
Which crouching seemed to float and swim,

Like a black dream through guilty sleep,—
A nightmare weighing on the sense,
Which strives, with hideous impotence,
To loose its tentacles, and shake
Its arms aside, yet *cannot* wake.
A dusky, shapeless Shape, alas!
    What may the formless horror be?
As faint as breath upon a glass,
    Yet dreadful in reality.
It seemed a Nothing palpable;
    From every stem its life it drew,
Each waterdrop of it was full;
It permeated all the pool;
    Through all the hollow deeps it grew;
And yet it crouched and darkened *there*,
Embodied as a soul's despair.
Then, something in thee whispered, " Death!"
    Whereon, the lurking Dread arose,
    And wavered upward, and drew close,
As if to clasp thee.—And with breath
That sobbed for terror, the dark dream
Was broken, and the dawn's first beam
Low-glinting through the window stole,
And fell like quiet on thy soul.

And is thy dream forgotten quite ?
Ah, we are blinded in the light !
   Yet tempt no more the treacherous wave
      And let the floating lily be :
For the dark pitfalls of the grave
      Lie everywhere, and none may see.
      Nay ! what were that one flower to thee,
Which, plucked, would forfeit all delight ?
Think of thy vision in the night !

Alas ! it is forgotten clean
   Gone, with her slumber and the hour :
She only sees the silver sheen,
   She only thinks upon the flower.
And thou who shouldst be wiser, say,
Doth not the dweller by Cathay*
Teach well that flowers have oft beguiled
The hoary head, the grey-grown child ?
But, of those blooms of fonder grace
And larger beauty—Venus' race,
And whitely-purer than her dove—
Sweet household flowers of joy and love,

---

* In the Malay language, the same word signifies
" women " and " flowers."   F. W.

Whose tendrils twine around our hearts,
And snare us with a thousand arts,—
Was never one more warmly wooed
By lover in his melting mood,
Than were the lilies of the lake
    By that strange child, who stole away
From home and mother, for their sake,
    At morn, and noon, and set of day.

For there were lilies rosy-red;
    And there were lilies azure-blue;
And golden cups that seemed to shed
    A halo round, of sunny hue.
    And azure, gold, and crimson, drew
Her longing thoughts, her wistful eyes :
    Childlike, she loved each glowing hue,
And, earthlike, wafted yearning sighs
To an unpurchasable prize.
But most she loved those lilies, white
As moonbeams sleeping in the night
    Upon a still and quiet stream
Or snowy brows that woo the sight—
And win it, too—'mid gauzes white
    And lucent as the paly beam
Of northern lights through which the pole
Looks steadfast as a constant soul.

And she would sit beside the brink,
   And watch the lazy lilies float,—
Each slowly rise, and poise, and sink,
   On mimic seas a mimic boat,
Stirred by the circling swells which shook
Along the lake, from where the brook,
With hollow gurglings, and a gush
Of whirling sparks, flecked sedge and rush
With foamy churnings, and beyond
Died in wide ripplings on the pond.

It was a passion—such a one
As comes between us and the sun
Of full-orbed reason, breeding shades
Through which belated Fancy wades
As in a vision open-eyed,
Where nothing truly is descried,
But all things wear the far-off gleam,
The distant glory, of a dream.
E'en so the Lotos-Eaters, when
   They plucked the fateful, happy fruit,
And wandered from the world of men
   To shining regions far remote—
E'en so, a-swoon, they fixed their dim
   And golden-moted reveries

3

Upon some thought beyond the rim
  Of waking, harsh realities,
And saw it swell and grow to be
Earth, heaven, moon, stars, Infinity.

Yes ! 'twas a *passion*—one whose sway
Grew stronger o'er her, day by day ;
A wish, a longing 'twas, whose power
Waxed in her bosom, hour by hour.
In vain her mother's fond caress ;
  In vain her warning tales of him
Who lurked beneath the quietness
  Of the blue waters, grisly-grim :
In vain her vision of the night :
  In vain the vague, unbodied fear
Which lurked around her like a sprite,
  Yet drew her ever to the mere
With trembling fascination, such
  As feels a bird when, glitter-eyed,
The serpent charms her to the clutch
  Of his coiled rings, from flutterings wide.
Through all her thoughts and dreams they grew,
  The silver lilies of the lake :
Her life's magnetic pole, they drew
  Her spirit, sleeping or awake ;

Until her soul was set in them,
Her longing's mystic diadem.

And when the fresh and ruddy morn
    Blew keen, cool odours through the air,
As perceant as the rose's thorn,
    And fragrant as the roses were ;
And breezy clouds, like full-blown sails,
Drove down the current of the gales ;
And grasses waved, and rustling trees
Twinkled like starbeams in the breeze ;
Full oft, the sunny morning air
Caught brighter sunshine from her hair,
As, sitting by the grassy marge,
    She watched the trembling lilies shiver ;
When the breeze passed, and set the large
    Green leaves around them all a-quiver.

And often, too, when heavy noon
    With thickly-moted light the air
Filled to o'erflowing, and, a-swoon,
    All nature slumbered,——sitting there,
    Of sun, and heaven, and earth unware,
She watched the drowsy lilies nod
    With slow and sleepy motion o'er

The breathless pool, whose surface trod
　　No dimpling wind, from shore to shore.
And now she sate, at set of day,
　　As ever, trancèd on the shore—
Herself a bright, unbodied ray
　　Meshed in the grass, and bending o'er
　　The glassy water's mirror-floor,—
And watched the lolling lilies lie
　　At anchor in the quiet lake—
Bright planets that from sky to sky
　　Their rainbow-gleams of glory shake.

But ah ! that vexing blossom, where
　　The dragon-fly lay sleeping still—
So near, and yet so distant, there,—
It takes her longing all a-snare :
　　She uses all her little skill ;
And wooes, and smiles, and strives to clutch ;
And still it slideth from her touch.
Above, the death's-head moth, afar,
　　Low-whirring, cleaves the deepening sky,
And strives toward the evening star,
　　And, vainly striving, draws not nigh.
And still, beneath, the yearning child
　　Leans forward through the dusking hour ;
And still delight, unreconciled,
　　Eludes her, with the gliding flower.

And from the pathway of the wind
   The Wandering Angel looked below,
And heard her sighing, and behind,
   With folded wings, and light as snow,
Alit upon the printless sward,
And fixed his sad and deep regard
On this young daughter of the clay,
Sighing her happiness away.

" And thus," he said, " the flickering shadow
   Darkens the face of Truth, alas !
The shades wide-billowing o'er a meadow,
   When breezes bend the bladed grass,
   The breath that thins from off a glass ;
   Do scarce more lightly fade and pass
Than the swift fancies human things
Pursue with such unequal wings."

And then he bent a weeping face
   Between his waving wings, which cast
A mournful splendour o'er thè place,—
   The gleam as of a happy Past
Seen through a light, half smiles, half tears,
Down the long vista of the years—
And, self-communing, seemed to be
Lost in some dim perplexity.

Anon, he raised his shining head,
   And, stretching a celestial hand,
" Yet 'tis a harmless wish," he said ;
    " And who should seek to understand
Why hearts will yearn to certain ends ?
It is enough the Maker bends
All things to wisest purposes.
   And thou, who yearnest for the flower,
Have, then, thy wish ; and only press
   Me to thy bosom through one hour,
(If for so long thy joy may live),
And I shall deem it blest to give."

And now the child, outwearied quite
   With longings vain, and vain endeavour,
Sat still, and watched the moonlike light
   Of the white petals glint and quiver,
More softly-toned and undefined,
Against the deepening disc behind.
And lo, upon her dream there stole
A tender cloud ; and o'er her soul
A soft and sleepy sadness grew,
As if the lotos' drowsy dew
Had drenched her with its slumberous spell ;
And o'er her senses gliding fell

A vague and dim presentiment,—
  A silver mist of melancholy,
  The feeling of a Presence holy,
The echo of a whisper sent
From far-off regions, to her heart—
A voice that said, " Arise ! depart !"
A thrilling whisper, low, intense ;
A tongue unknown, yet fraught with sense.
It was not fear that shook her so—
Her sadness had no touch of woe;
But from the Unknown came a breath ;
  And o'er the mystic bridge of Time
She heard, half 'ware, the feet of Death
  Pace nearer from the shadowy clime—
Pass outward toward her from that bourne
O'er which no traveller doth return.
As in a dream she seemed to see
  The lake before her glint and glimmer ;
And heard the rustle of the tree,
And the grass creep along the lea ;
  And saw the faint eve shift and shimmer
  To palier beams, and duskings dimmer ;
And, far away, the Night drop down
Through gleaming deeps, from realms unknown.

But while she dreameth, lo ! beside
    The very margin rises up,—
Heaving a ripple slow and wide,—
    A moonlike disc, a silver cup ;
A lily, lovelier far than those
She yearneth for—a flower that glows,
As with an innate glory, through
The deepening eve, and hung with dew,
Whose little twinkling globules are,
Each in itself a mimic star.
She starts, she wakens at the sight,
    She clasps her infant hands with joy—
Young heiress to a rich delight,
    Full-golden, drossed with no alloy.
All she forgot, no more she hears
That silent voice from other spheres ;
The muffled tread of pacing Death ;
The stifled sigh, the Unknown's breath..
She only sees the flower before her,
    She only hears her heart sing loud ;
She only feels delight stoop o'er her,
    And clasp her like a rosy cloud.

She need but lean forth from the strand,
She need but stretch her little hand,

And grasp the yielding stem, and draw
  The nectarous goblet lightly in :
    Yet sate she still upon the shore
    While, tranced, her spirit hovered o'er
The regal blossom, dashed with awe.—
It seemed too great a prize to win !

But now, adown the winding dell,
  From where it meets the upland meadows,
  A silvery voice athwart the shadows,
Like a dove wounded, fluttering fell.
A woman's voice, a mother's cry,
  It trembled down the trembling air,
And woke a plaintive, sweet reply,
  Like the low response of a prayer,
  From cavern-echoes sleeping there :—
" My child ! my life of life ! my star !
  Where art thou, love ? where hidest thou ?
For now the Powers of Evil are
  Abroad—the Death is walking now :
The wicked Genie now doth wake ;
  The treacherous pool grows dark and chilly.
Say, dost thou sit beside the lake,
  And look upon the floating lily ? "

Again she starts :—her mother's voice !
  And sweet her mother's voice should be :
But now, it threatens at her joys,
  It jars upon her ecstasy.
For lo ! she comes, with fearful care,
  To lead her homeward through the eve,
And leave her spirit floating there
  Above the floating flower, to grieve
For incomplete delights, which turn
So sour in Sorrow's yeasty urn.
No ! no ! the flower is at her feet—
She need but stoop to gather it.

And once again the mother cries,
" My child ! Lone starlight of mine eyes !
Oh ! dost thou watch the lilies shake
Upon the deep and treacherous lake ? "

Now, now, or never, seize the flower,
For chance is fleeter than the hour ;
And he who waits on time shall see
That power is mutability.
She bendeth o'er the mirror wide ;
  She stoops above the gleaming glass ;
  She holds not by the tufted grass,

Nor by the wild vine close beside :
Who, with the goblet at his lip,
Feared ever, yet, lest it should slip ?

And yet once more the mother calls
While the low sunset further falls,
And deepen far eve's orient halls :
" My child ! my star ! where art thou, sweet ?
Dim shadows waver round my feet :
Dim terrors at my bosom beat.
My heart ! my soul's identity !
Thy doting mother yearns for thee :
My child ! my star ! O answer me ! "

And, panting, kin to raptures wild,
And leaning farther out, the child
Shook her young voice's folded flower
In sweetness through the dewy hour :
  " I am here : *
   O come near !
   I, your star,
   Am not far ;
   Am not ——"

---

* These words of the child's reply are not mine. They occur in the
original Tale, but in a prose form.   F. W.

And then, it closed again—
The dewy blossom of her speech ;
Though the faint echoes of the glen
    Kept softly babbling, each to each,
The lovely tones, so sweet and clear ;
    Until their drowsy murmurs died
    In the wild warblings shaken wide
    From where the streamlet's whirling tide.
Gushed out upon the lilied mere.

And silence, like a terror, fell
Down all the windings of the dell.
But from the lake a sudden surge
    Arose, and beat the wounded grass,
And strewed it broken round the verge,
And moaned and muttered like a dirge,
    And sobbed and sighed, Alas ! alas !
And, far within the deepening sky,
The evening planet closed its eye,
And died into the wreath of cloud
Which trailed around it like a shroud.

Is it a falling star whose wake
Gleams broadened o'er the heaving lake ?
Or the full moon's reflection, spread

By many a wavelet's glancing head?
And do the evening breezes shake
These sudden surges o'er the lake?
And what is yon dim shade, which creeps
Slow-wavering upward from the deeps?
Was it the blackbird's pipe I heard?
And yet he is an early bird:
Or the shrill sparrow passing by?
Or the lone lapwing's mournful cry?

Alas! no meteor slides o'erhead,
   Nor any image spreads below:
The moon is only crescented;
   And she is faint, and, hanging low,
Has scarcely cleared the summit yet
Of the far mountain-parapet.
The evening zephyr is abroad,
   But not the moths more lightly skim—
The slender grasses scarcely nod
   Their plumy heads of seed to him.
The blackbird is not nested here,—
Why should he linger by the mere?
Nor did the sparrow flutter by;
Nor did the lonely lapwing cry.

But where is she who sat so late,
　　All panting, by the lakelet's brink?
The spot is vacant where she sate;
　　She hath evanished, like a blink
　　Of starlight ere the mind can think—
Gone, like the summer-lightning's gleam;
Passed, like a sweet but transient dream!

Ah! hideous vision of the night!
　　Ah! dreadful dream, so dreadly crowned!
He hath her, see! the Evil Sprite—
　　The formless Shadow clasps her round!
He blinds her eyes—he sucks her breath—
She stiffens in the grasp of Death.

For, as she bent above the bloom,
Fate stole upon her through the gloom,
And smote her treacherously behind;
　　Till, shaken rudely on the tree
Of Life, by that ungentle wind,
　　Her little blossom quiveringly
　　Writhed a moment—floated free—
　　And dropt into Eternity.

She over-reached in eagerness;
　　And poising like a sunbeam there,

One instant, in her keen distress,
  Beat with her little palms the air ;
Then fell upon the floating lily,
  And, like a lily, floating yet,
Gleamed whitely on the waters chilly,
  The fairest blossom in them set.
And, startled from his slumbers nigh,
Up sprang the shining dragon-fly,
And hovered for a moment on
  His swift, invisible wings ; then wheeled ;
And, darting sideways, he is gone,
  Swift as the shadow o'er a field.
And then the formless Shadow rose,
And wavered upward, and crept close,
And froze the cry upon her lips,
  And drenched her floating dress, and drew
Her down through darkness and eclipse :
  And o'er her closed the waters blue :
And but the bubbles of her breath,
  The oily eddy whirling slow,
And the tost lily, showed where Death
  Had dragged her to the shades below.

Full silence now—a perfect round,
And broken by no flaw of sound ;

Unless it be the gurgling hiss,
Which marks it like an emphasis,
From where the lake and streamlet meet,
Like lovers vext, with chidings sweet ;
Or the dew dripping from a flower ;
   Or, far within the rosy bosk,
A turtle, settling to her bower,
   Who murmurs in her green kiosk.

But hark ! a footstep on the slopes,
Light as a flying antelope's ;
The flutter of a waving dress
   Amid the waving fern above ;
A figure winged by swift distress,
   A mother's footsteps winged with love.
She comes, a woman beautiful
   As Eden's Eva, ere she fell :
She glides, a moonbeam, toward the pool—
She floats, an angel, through the cool
   Dim air of evening, down the dell.
She cannot see the margin yet,
   For the tall cypress rising near,
And showing now a cone of jet
   Against the purple atmosphere,
Save where the quivering western ray

Slopes upward through the widening vale,
And tips with fire its topmost spray,
  Far-gleaming through the twilight pale.
She cannot see—and it is well :
  For where is she who called so late ?
And broken grass and flowers can spell
  A fearful chronicle of Fate.

But ere her white and twinkling feet,
  Though swift as arrowy beams, could mete
The space betwixt her and the shore,
  The lilies, open-eyed for awe,
  A sight of marvel dimly saw :
For through the lakelet's shining floor
A blackbird passed into the air,
  Upborne on whistling pinions flew,
And lighting on the cypress, there
  From her dank plumage shook the dew, *
Until the glittering shower fell
Like swarming fireflies down the dell :
And still she threeped and wailed, and shook
  The little feathers on her throat,
Till it was tremulous as the brook,
  And poured as thickly note on note.

---

* " And from his dank plume dashed the dew."—SCOTT, Rokeby C.I

4

And now the mother, flitting down,
  Around the dusky copses flew ;
And, as she passed, her fluttering gown,
  Dashed out the little lamps of dew
Star-loving Vesper 'gan to trim
And kindle through his bowers dim :
And so, until she reached the shore,
With the last daylight glinting o'er ;
And the low-lying lake, a-gleam
Like some vague fancy through a dream.
And, brighter than the diamond dews,
  And deeper than the skies above,
And warmer than the sunset hues,

  The dawn of joy, the light of love,
Which through her deep and liquid eyes
Rose broadening up,—the soul's sunrise.
For there she sate beside the marge,—

  Her life, her love, her own sweet lily,
And looked upon the fairy barge
  At anchor on the water chilly :
Her own fair child, and safe from harm ;
  Her morning and her evening star,
With quick life-flushes rosy-warm
  As yon rich evening tinctures are.

O blissful balm to pricking fears !
O roguish joy, disguised in tears !
With tearful smiles, and tender blame,
And quick, fond feet the mother came ;
And, bending o'er her treasure, threw
  An arm around the slender waist ;
And took the little hands, and drew
    To meet and still her throbbing breast ;
    And stroked the golden curls, and prest
    The shining head in that sweet nest
Whose swell had been its lullaby
In days that yet were scarce gone by.
And ah ! what dove could emulate
Those murmurs half-articulate,—
The random speech of tenderness,
  Yet fraught so full of meaning, too ;
Soft wordless cooings, which express
  The heart, as words could never do.
And ah ! the hungry love that feeds
  On swift caresses, warm and wild,
And still from food a hunger breeds :—
  O happy mother ! happy child !

But now, her first delight subsides—
Her swelling rapture's stormy tides

Ebb to that full-brimmed happiness
Whose volume yet is none the less,
But, levelled down to broad content,
Lies lower, yet hath more extent.
And then, as one who, hunger-faint,
   Set down before a plenteous feast,
Binds appetite to no restraint,
   But lets it range from west to east,
And north to south, of full desire,
As ravenous as a prairie's fire ;
   Until, its first keen edge appeased,
It grows more dainty-delicate,
   Contracts its circle, and refines,—
He toys with that and the other cate
   And tastes and sips the costly wines :
So. now, her first fond frenzy o'er,
   Her first love-hunger reconciled,
   The mother bent above her child,
To taste love's sweets at leisure more ;
And, bending back the graceful head,
   And stroking down the golden hair,
Looked on the lovely face, and fed
   Her heart, like bees on honey, there.

But, while she looked and feasted, lo !
   O'er the deep heaven of her eyes
A cloud, a shadow, gathered slow—
   The vapour of a vague surmise,
   A dim and unfulfilled surprise :
The feeling of a Want unknown,—
   Impalpable as are these swells
Of fairy music zephyr-blown
   From the slim hyacinth's swinging bells.
For, in the face that looked on hers,
   An immaterial, lurking change
Through all her throbbing bosom stirs
   A sudden discord, harsh and strange :
Some subtle tint of difference,
   As rarefied, as airy-fine,
   As where the rainbow, line on line,
Mingles its bands beyond the sense.
It seems her child, yet not her child—
   The same in every feature fair ;
And thus she ever looked and smiled :
   Yet there is *something* wanting there.

And in her veins the blood began
To freeze and curdle as it ran ;
And, creeping slowly o'er her head,
She felt the hair rise, stiff with dread :

For, like a weeping cloud of dew,
A cold and clammy terror grew,
  Condensing in her chilly breast;
And a voice whispered, " Danger," near ;
  And sudden waves of swift unrest,
From all the heavy atmosphere,
Beat at the barriers of her heart,
And rent its ocean-walls apart,
Builded so late by Joy and Love,
  And plucked them from their rooted strength;
And, pouring darkly inward, drove
  Peace from her mind, through all its length.

And then (for Fear is Argus-eyed),
  She cast a trembling glance around,
And through the gloaming first descried
  The bubbly froth that flecked the ground
Where the vext lake had risen, and spat
  Its churnèd spume upon the shore ;
And saw the grasses trampled flat,
  And many a wild flower scattered o'er.
And to her heart there struck a pain
  More cold than ice, more cold than death ;
    And from her life there seemed to pass,
    (Like the reflection from the glass),

Something that seemed a part of breath
Ne'er to be breathed whole again.

Yet turned she to the child, who sate,
And seemed to watch her looks, amate ;
And, with a voice whose accents shook
As throughly as the tremulous brook,
"O Sweet," she said,—and it was strange,
    And very pitiful, to note
In the soft tones a chill of change,
    Ev'n while they fondly strove to dote—
"O Sweet ! what ravage here hath set
    The rugged imprint of its foot ?
For all the grass is bruised and wet,
    As far as to the cypress' root ;
And many a wild-flower broken lies ;
    And, see ! the foam has flecked the shore,
All round, with many little eyes,
    And drenched the earth through every pore.
But thou, my Life, art dry and warm :
And yet—ah ! yet—a dim alarm
Whispers my soul of hidden harm.
O say, my child, what this may be :
Look up, my love, and answer me."

Then, as a lily sways and dips
　　In veering flaws, her snowy hand
With sudden pressure sealed the lips
　　That would have answered her demand:
And, "Hush! yet hush!" she cried, and bent
　　Above the child, and raised her up;
"Why should I care for Fate's intent
　　If still the wine is in my cup?
I have thee—have I *not ?*—my Star!
　　Yes! yes! I feel thee at my breast.
Oh! let us haste and fly afar
　　From the cold lake, where fear doth rest."

She said; she turned; she poised for flight,
　　As doth a frayed and startled dove;
When, from the fiery cone of light
　　Which topt the cypress, high above,
The blackbird shook a sudden shower
　　Of wailing notes adown the dell,
Which, like the petals of a flower
　　By storm-winds scattered, floating fell
In fluttering spirals, through the air—
　　A wild, and sweet, and mournful strain,
With lurking echoes of despair,
　　And long, long, shrilling cries of pain.

She paused, on tiptoe trembling still,
  Like a white moonbeam through the shade,
And felt the flooding music fill
  Her bosom, as it brimmed the glade :
She sank upon the tender palms
  Of her small feet, and rooted stood,
Still as a lily in the calms
  That overflow the summer wood.
O blackbird singing to the eve !
  O little chorister of woe !
What makes thy pulsing bosom heave
  With such a wild, impassioned throe ?
It shakes the feathers on its throat,
  It ruffles up the quiet air,
Till, rippling out in rings remote,
  The storm of song is driven there,
  In rocking eddies of despair,
In gusts of deep, delicious pain,
  In whirlwind sighs of sorrow, borne
Adown the glen, across the plain,
  And from the evening to the morn.

And *she*—she stood, and breathed in
Each note, quick, piercing, crystalline ;
And every note seemed still to pierce,

With a fine fury, keen and fierce,
Her soul, as light the universe.
And on her breast she felt her daughter
Tremble—as doth a quiet water,
When rain-storms beat upon its bosom—
'Neath the song-shower ; or as a blossom,
When adverse breezes beat the bough,
 And set it quivering 'twixt their poise ;
Or as a bird, which hears below
 The sudden shout of climbing boys,
And stretching o'er the nest-edge, sees
Them climbing nearer by degrees.

And now, the haunting doubt took shape :
 And the division in her heart
Yawned widely to a rugged gap,
 Where her affection stood apart
On this, the near side, and, on that,
Her bleeding, broken will lay flat.
For now the child, who never yet
Felt in her arms a feather-weight,
Seems heavier grown ; or is't that Love
 Who bore the burthen till to-day,
Is weaklier now, and cannot move
 Such strength of spirit in the clay ?

And then the bird that sings so sweet !—
She thrills from forehead down to feet ;
 It draws her very heart away—
And can it be that it shall steal
 Affection, by a song beguiled?
And can it be that she shall feel
 More for the bird than for her child?
She fears it all !—yea ! while she stands,
She feels her heart unloose its bands,
And vainly strives to hold it back
By many strings that rend and crack,
Till it breaks free, and floats away
Into the light of dying day,
Into the cypress-top, and clings
Around the blackbird as it sings.
And heavier on her bosom yet
She feels the child more deeply fret,
And hates herself that she should let
One thought rebel against a weight
So more than dear so very late.

And so she stood, and so she hearkened,
 And so she strove with love and will,
Till the short twilight o'er her darkened,
 And the large dew shone round and chill.

And not until the bird had ceased,
And, trembling from the purple east,
The slowly-sloping moonbeams fell
With sharper slant into the dell,
Piercing the bosks with many a lance,
Did she emerge from her deep trance.
But then, she seemed to waken slowly,
   As from a dimly-dreaming sleep,
Peopled with shades of melancholy ;
   And felt her blood thick-curdling creep ;.
And looked from 'neath a heavy lid
To where the gleaming pyramid
Of the tall cypress clave the night,
But silvered, now, with softer light ;
And strained her eyes, and strove to see
   If yet the bird were perchèd there .
But nothing stirred upon the tree,
   Nor any motion vext the air.

And then she heaved a heavy sigh,
   And bent above the quiet child,
   Who had not moved, nor spoke, nor smiled,.
Through all her trance, but kept an eye
Of more than childish meaning fixed
Upon the changing moods that mixed

And fluttered in her countenance :
And, meeting now that large, deep glance,
The mother shuddered to her soul,
   Beneath a dim and nameless dread,
As the ship driven on a shoal
   Quivers from keel to mainmast-head.
Yet none the less she bent, and kissed
The fair young brow, and through a mist
Of swimming teardrops sadly smiled,
With struggling fondness, on the child :
Then, shook her head, and sighed, and said,
   But in a low and stifled voice,
" Cling close, my Star ! for day has shed
   His golden petals ; and rejoice
The Powers of Evil in the night :
Ah, Sweet ! we have outstayed the light."
Then, slowly moved athwart the gloom,
   And thridded round the dusky bosk,
     With many a wistful glance behind ;
And vaguely felt the moist perfume
   Of roses, violets, and musk,
     Mingle upon the heavy wind.
So, up the slope, and through the shadows,
Till on the margin of the meadows
She gleamed one moment, like a ray
Of the pale moon, then passed away.

And, all night long, the moaning lake
   Was shaken by a sobbing wind ;
And all the lilies lay awake,
   And stared upon the darkness blind
With lidless eyes, until the dawn
Looked pale o'er stream, and copse, and lawn.

*   *   *   *   *   *   *   *

How fares it with the mother's heart,
   Since that disastrous hour
In which her being seemed to part
   The honey of its flower ?
Alas ! not she herself can tell;
   For all her feelings seem to be
Writ in a cypher, which to spell
   To any sense, she holds no key.
Her daughter plays about the door,
Or, like a sunbeam, trips the floor ;
Nor doth she wander any more
 To watch the lilies from the shore.
But still within the mother's breast
Forever sate the veiled Unrest ;
And through her spirit's inner gloom
She seemed to see an open tomb,
Beside whose brink stood muffled Care ;
And love and joy were buried there.

She strove—*so hard*—to love her child,
  But still her yearning thoughts would stray ;
And evermore, her heart, beguiled
  By some vague power, would range away,
And like the water-lilies shake
And tremble o'er the quiet lake.
She strove to hearken for that voice
  Which in more happy days had been
The little herald of her joys ;
  But still, her ear and it between,
Flowed in the memory of that song
Wailing the twilight glade along.

And often, she would drop her face
  Between her trembling palms, and weep,
And hate herself that she should pace
  An alien shore of heart, and steep
Her spirit in an alien wave
Of love, and make that breast the grave
Of sweet affections, which should be,
Instead, their dearest nursery.
But all in vain !—the void was there,
  The Shadow loomed beside the hearth ;
Nor could she drive it forth, nor rear
  Her fallen love again from earth.

But, ever, when the evening fell
Along the meads and down the dell,
And when the sunset round the west
　　Flowed widely, like a sea of blood,
And, in the east, upon the crest
　　Of the dim hills, pale twilight stood,
And looked upon the dying day,
And darkened, as he past away,—
Then, when the hour's similitude
　　Was strongest to that other eve
When first the soul within her blood
　　Began to pine, and droop, and grieve,
Would she steal softly to the door,
　　And, leaning 'twixt the lights and shadows,
　　Strain a quick ear across the meadows,
To hear if from the lakelet's shore
Swelled up that song to which her soul
Shook, as the needle to the pole.

And ever, when the evening dew
　　Filled its first spheres upon the grass,
And—whence the valley oped the view
　　To westward, down the winding pass—
When the long beams sloped slowly up,
　　And, ever rising high and higher,

Smote full upon the cypress-top,
  And turned it to a cone of fire,
The blackbird, sitting in the glow,
  Would swell her little feathered throat,
And pour her notes around, below,
  And to the evening far remote—
A cry of wail, a wailing cry,
  A voice of sorrow, wild, forlorn,
That plained along the earth and sky,
  And from the evening to the morn.

And when the mother, at her door,
  Heard the first echoes of the song,
She waited not for palampore,
  Nor threw the yashmak's veil along
Her sadly-brightening face ; but turned
  To see if yet her daughter slept ;
Then sighed, and with a heart that yearned
  To reach the valley, gliding stept
Light as a fawn, across the lea,
  And through the shimmering mists of even,
And through the faint obscurity
  That crept along the deepening heaven ;
And down the slope, and round the copse,
Beneath the rose-trees' fragrant tops,
With little crimson lamps hung o'er ;
  5

And so, until she reached the shore,
And stood beneath the cypress tree,
  And saw askant the water-lily
At anchor on its mimic sea,
  And the low lakelet glinting chilly..

And there, as in a trancèd dream,
  She listened to the wailing bird,
Till upward slid the western beam,
  And died away, and moaning stirred
The dim nightwind amid the shade,
  And, tracing wavy lines of light,
The glancing fireflies filled the glade,
  And the stars twinkled full and bright.
And then she woke, and sighed again,
  And passed, with many a glance behind,
And left the valley to the reign
  Of darkness and the sobbing wind.

And, all the while, the child, at home,
  Upon her little bed would sit,
And watch the shadows go and come,
  And the bats fly, and owlets flit:
And in her large eyes shone the gleam

As of a sorrow lurking deep,
Like shades that flicker in a stream,
　Or heavy dreams that darken sleep :
Until the mother's stealthy tread
　Came creeping softly to the door—
Then stretched upon her little bed,
　And seemed to sleep and dream once more.

Now many days have come and gone,
Till the rich autumn draweth on ;
And all the woods wear favours strange,
　And alter with the altered time,
But only to such temperate change
　As marks alone that sunny clime.
But more than outward nature's hue
　Was changed within the mother's breast :
There, chillier blasts of sorrow blew ;
　There, withered leaves of love, and rest,
And genial pleasure, thicklier fell ;
Until her heart was as a well
Choked by the foliage dank and sere
Of all that makes our being dear.

Her heart is farther from her child :
　She loves it not—she *cannot* love !

No ! not though she, with passion wild,
   Has striven to dote, in vain she strove.
For ever, still, the b'ackbird's song
   Is wailing in her ear, and draws
Her spirit so, that, right or wrong,
   She cannot stop, she cannot pause,
   She cannot reason to a cause ;
But, woman-like and mother-like,
There, where her deep affections strike,
   They thrive, obeying native laws.
And daily colder grew her kiss,
   And still, more careless waxed her care ;
Nor, if 'twere absent, did she miss
   The child, nor any sunbeam there.

But ah ! she loved the lonely bird,—
   Loved it too fondly and too well ;
Or so she deemed : her love was stirred
   And swayed as by some potent spell.
From day to day the passion grew ;
   And still, from eve to eve, she went
Through twilight and the glittering dew,
   To hear the wailing bird lament ;
Nor longer thought upon the child,
   Nor looked nor hearkened if it slept :

Yet often, too, she moaned and wept,
And beat her breast in sorrow wild,
And called herself a wretch, who could
So dwindle from her own sweet blood.
And thus she slid from wave to wave
 Of restless thought, and dark unrest ;
And, evermore, the open grave
 Yawned darker, grimlier, in her breast.

And now the woods are lean and pale,
 And wan and withered look the leaves,
And thickly shower they in the gale
 That blows from winter's icy eaves.
And, in the dell, the rose-trees now
 Have shaken out their little lamps
In crimson flakes of flame, that blow
 O'er earth and air, until the damps
Of spongy ground and clammy grass
Ensnare and stop them, as they pass,
And slowly quench their waning fire
With chilly dews and cloggy mire.
And on the darkening slopes around,
 The summer flowers were dead or dying ;
Half-buried in the plashy ground,
 Or drooping low, or lowly lying,

And rotting into many a hue
Of cold corruption—black, and blue,
And purple, red, and that moist yellow
Which marks the corpse when maggot-mellow.
And on the lake the lilies fell
   In showers of crimson, gold, and blue,
And sickly white ; and every swell
   That shook the ruffled water through,
Drove them about from side to side,
And whirled them into eddies wide,
And dashed them on the shore, till they
Melted to pulp, and oozed away.
But, of the hardier, still a few
Clung to their stalks, and weathered through
The rugged hours, with steadfast eyes
Fixed on the dun, inclement skies ;
   As though a whisper from the root
   Through all their branching veins might shoot—
" Ah ! yes : to-day the blossom dies.
But spring will come, and we shall rise."
And all was changed, and darker grown,
   Save for the willow hoary-grey,
Who darkened o'er the wave alone —
   But he looked never green nor gay—

And the tall cypress' sombre spire,
Lent to no changing season's hire.

*   *   *   *   *   *   *   *

And in the fading of the year
   How fares it with the mother now ?
As in a nightmare dim and drear,
   She feels a weight upon her brow,
She feels a burthen at her heart,
   She feels a load upon her breast ;
And strives to fling that load apart,
   Yet cannot break her restless rest.
And ah ! how changed and faded now !
Pale is the lily on her brow,
And pale the downy cheek, and white
   And wasted is the delicate hand,
Till you can almost see the light
   Shine through it, and the slow blood stand
Along those blue and branching stains
Which mark the courses of the veins.
And though her lips are dewy yet—
   Sweet lips but made to kiss and smile !—
Still seems it as if Death had set
   His seal on their twin rose the while,
And nipt it with his icy gale,
So cold they are, so still, so pale.

But saddest, 'neath their ebon bars,
　　Those orbs of deep and liquid light,—
Those eyes that shine like lonely stars
　　Far-wandered from their orbits bright,
　　And lost in dim abysms of night.
For through them burned a wasting fire,
　　Clipt round and swallowed up in dark,
As, when the moon and stars expire
　　'Neath rolling clouds, the steady spark
Of some lone lamp that lights a tomb
Gleams through the unreflecting gloom.
And in them lurked a hungry want,—
　　A look that ever seemed to seek
Some dream her slumber would not grant,
　　Some wish she could not frame to speak,
Some viewless vision of the air,
Which fluttered round her unaware,
Thin as the wind within her hair,
Yet palpable as it, and strong
To draw her breaking heart along.

Her breaking heart—for it *was* breaking,
　　Swiftly and surely, day by day:
The storms within it ever shaking,
The throbs as of a shock earthquaking,
　　Crumbled and rent the fragile clay ;

Until from every widened pore
The soul looked forth, and strove to soar.

And, when the mother thought not on it,
 The child upon her wasted face
Would fix sad eyes, and sadly con it,
 O'er all its changed but deathless grace ;
Then deeply sigh, and turn away,
And make pretence to sport and play :
But, when the mother was away,
Sate still, from end to end of day,
And darkly watched the slow hours slide
O'er the round world's revolving side.

But not of her the mother thought ;
 Except when, sometimes, suddenly,
Remorse within her spirit wrought,
 And she would drop upon her knee,
And clasp and kiss her little daughter,
And tremble like a running water,
And shed such tears as scald the heart
From which their fiery fountains start,
And strive to speak through sobbings quick,
And choke her words in accents thick :
Until the tempest, rolling o'er,
Left her as lifeless as before.

But rare such moods, and far between ;
 And rarer, farther, daily grew :
For, as her being's latest scene
 In life's dark drama nearer drew,
The blackbird and its wailing song
 Filled all her narrowing stage of time—
The crescent passion waxed more strong,
 And rounded to its perfect prime :
A moon of love, that swayed the wide
 Deep sea of feeling to its power,
And ruled its motions and its tide—
 The planet of her closing hour.

And, though her step was feeble now,
 And though the hectic on her cheek
Showed where, 'neath death's horizon-brow,
 The dawn of Life indeed 'gan break ;
Still through the weeping dew and dusk
 And shimmering evening-mist, she went,
And down the slope, and round the bosk,
 To hear the lonely bird's lament ;
And stood beneath the cypress tree,
 And saw, askant, the lingering lily
Shiver upon its wintry sea,
And the low lake glint dark and chilly.

For still the cypress' cone of jet
  Clave up the the twilight sombre-grey ;
And still eternal Nature set
  Its peak afire, at fall of day ;
And still the blackbird, from the glow,
Shook its wild song around, below ;
And shrilled its passion and its pain,
  In wailing cries, in sobs forlorn,
Adown the glen, across the plain,
  And from the evening to the morn.

The dawn is lightening, loath and low ;
  The light is spreading, chill and grey ;
The day is breaking, sad and slow ;
  And heavily the heavy ray
Shoots forth from heaven's cloudy lids
Through the far mountain pyramids ;
And, all along the upland wealds,
  And all along the glimmering meadows,
And o'er the woods, and groves, and fields,
  And winding streams, the sullen shadows
Slowly retreat, and lingering war
Against the crested morning star.
The dews are dense on blade and leaf,
  And palely shimmer in the light

Those tears that tell the peri's grief,
  Who weepeth only through the night.
And from the low horizon-verge
  Sweeps up a sad and mourning wind,
And passes onward, like a dirge,
  Into the western shadows blind.
A cheerless morning, dim, and cold :
And yet some tints of burning gold
Which kindle on those clouds uprolled
Above the mountains far away,
Hint that this dawn so chill and grey
May usher in a lovely day.

But see ! along the lonely meadows,
Far out, just where the wavering shadows.
Flicker upon the gentle swell
That slopes into the lily-dell,
What figure moves along the lea ?
A ray 'mid the obscurity ;
A sunny flash of golden hair :
Is it the child who wanders there ?
And does the old desire once more
  Drive sleep away, and bid her wake,.
To watch the lilies, from the shore,
  At anchor on the quiet lake ?

It *is* the child : but no desire
  Of lake or lily draws her now :
A motive holier and higher
  Is at her heart ; and o'er her brow
A shade of pensive thought is hung,
Too serious, sure, for one so young.
It is the child :—All night, awake,
  She sate upon her little bed,
To hear, returning from the lake,
  Her mother's faint and faltering tread.
All night she sate, all night she hearkened,
While the still hours around her darkened,
And the slow meteors sliding drew
Long wakes of fire athwart the blue :
But nothing moved upon the lea,
  No footstep crept across the flats ;
    Nor any stir nor voice she heard
    But, hooting shrill, the nightly bird,
The raven croaking dismally,
  And the quick flitting of the bats.

And now, at earliest peep of dawn,
  She hath arisen from her bed,
And crept across the dewy lawn,
  And o'er the meadow wanderèd,—

To where, above the eastern swell,
  The waving shadows flickering shake,
And the stream brawls adown the dell,—
  To seek her mother by the lake.
For well she knows, if, anywhere,
That mother breathes the vital air,
And looks upon the morning, she
Will find her near the cypress-tree ;
For, where the heart, the frame will be,.
If Love and Possibility
Pace on a par through twin degree.

And so, she glides adown the slope,
  Among the withered flowers and fern ;
And sees the cypress' dusky cope
  Pierce the white dawning, dark and stern ;.
And marks a sudden turning ope
A crescent glimmer of the lake,
Where one pale lily lies awake,
And, just beyond, the willow gleam
Athwart the archway of the stream ;
  But nothing further can discern.

And now she gains the lower vale,
  And slowly thrids the shadowy bosks,.
Half glimmering into morning pale,
  And half submerged in weeping dusks ;

Nor longer sweet with blowing musks,
But lean of leaf, and bristling o'er
   With thorns that weakly ward the tusks
Of winter's rugged northern boar.
And all is silent in the dell,
   Save only for the moaning wind
That passes with a heavy swell,
   And leaves a heavy pause behind ;
And a wave wapping on the shore,
Where the vext lakelet, spilling o'er
Its chilly margin, beats the bands
Of pebbly beach, like drowning hands
That grasp at Time in agony,
Yet sink into Eternity ;
And the wild rivulet, where it grieves
   And mutters like a dim despair ;
And the low whisper of the leaves,
   A-shiver in the morning air.
No other sound : for yet has stirred
Not even that early morning-bird
Who welcomes in the coming light,
   And takes the glory on his wings,
Far-soaring into regions bright,
   And singing soars, and soaring sings. *

---

* See Shelley's " Ode to a Skylark."

And now, at length, she doth emerge,
   Beyond the final curve of copse,
Close to the water's chilly verge,
   And where the sombre cypress tops
Those musk-rose alleys, glades, and groves,
The summer haunt of cooing doves,
But empty now, and silent all,
As is the mansion funeral ;
And turneth toward the cypress tree,—
   But all is still and voiceless there ;
And drops her eyes ; and, suddenly,
   Breaks up the quiet morning air,
And the brief silence of its reign,
With a low, stifled cry of pain ;
Then claspt her hands, and stilly stood,
And pale through all her pausing blood.

For there, beside the cypress' foot,
   White as her snowy robe, she lay !
A lovely statue, cold and mute ;
   A beauteous form of moulded clay :
Her head is on the mossy root,
   And, stretched in graceful curves away,
Her rounded limbs and figure lie,
As if in slumber, quietly.

Her hyacinthine hair, unbound,
Flows in dark billows o'er the ground :
And o'er that calm, unthrobbing breast,
   No longer fluttered by the breath
Of careful life, one hand is prest,
   As fondling something underneath ;
And by her side, with open palm,
The other lies in gracious calm.

And sooth, she only seems to sleep,
   She looks so calm, so graceful lies ;
And, as in slumber sweet and deep,
   Her lids are drooped above her eyes ;
And those sweet lips, that half-unclose,
   As if in tender-taken breath,
Have shed not yet their dewy rose
   Unto the frozen kiss of Death.
And though that brow and cheek are white
As was the dawning's paly light,
Not on them sits that livid gloom—
The awful herald of the tomb ;
But smooth they show, and soft, and fair,
As yonder lilies lately were.

And nothing, save that marble breast,
No longer heaving through the vest ;
  6

And that dread silence which no breath
Of lightest being fluttereth ;
And the sad, subtle, nameless air
   Which marks a spirit passed away,
Proclaim, indeed, that Azrael there
   Hath set his seal on soulless clay,
And that those eyes, so darkly fringed,
Shall never more be passion-tinged,
   Nor ever see yon rising day.

But lo ! the child :—She stands beside,
   And weepeth not as children do ;
For every separate tear doth slide,
   Slow, large, and round, from wells of dew
   That lie below the line of view.
Nor doth she sob, and wring her hands,
   And shriek, as children in distress ;
But very quietly she stands,
And grave, as one who understands
   Death, and its awful holiness :
Silent she stands, and voiceless weeps,
While the slow morning upward creeps.

Anon, she wakens from her trance,
And shakes the mist from her deep glance,

And bends above the lifeless breast,
  And, reverent-fingered, moves aside
The quiet hand, there lightly prest,
  And looks to see what it may hide.
And there *it* lay—the passionate bird !
  But silent, now, the thrilling tongue,
And, now, the throbbing throat unstirred,
  That still, at eve, so wildly sung ;
And cold the panting breast that lies
  Upon a bosom all as cold ;
And glazed, and sunk the large, dark eyes :—
  Its song is sung, its tale is told :
No more, at eve, its maddening strain
  In whirling eddies shall be borne
Adown the dell, along the plain,
  And from the evening to the morn.
It lies upon the heart it drew,
  Each eve, across the glimmering meadows,
And through the weeping dusk and dew,
  And through the falling chills and shadows.
They seemed to breathe a kindred breath
In life ; and they are kin in death.

But towering, waxed the altered form
  That bent above them, as they lay ;

And a great radiance, soft and warm,
  Broke in upon the tardy day—
A light of argent waving wings,
  A face of solemn pain and love;
And, like a dream's bright visitings,
  The Wandering Angel stood above.

And, " Rest," he said, " poor human hearts,
  The broken by my foolish dream:
For Fate will work HIS many parts,
  However men or angels deem.
I thought to yield an infant joy;
And lo! I lured but to destroy.
  thought to save a mother pain;
And lo! I pierced both heart and brain.
Soul of a mother! what may blind
Thy spiritual eye of mind?
Thy love, that seeketh, and will win,
Through darkness, death, and change, its kin?"

He spake; then bent, and gravely kissed
  That brow, at length so still and calm;
And softly took the pulseless wrist,
  And softly laid the tender palm

Back o'er the quiet bird, at rest
Forever in its native nest :
Then rose, and stretched a solemn hand
    Above, and blessed them as they lay ;
And raised his eyes above the land,
    And inly mourning seemed to pray :
Till level from the brightening east
    Shot on the courier beam of morn,
And, rising to his daily feast
    Of joy and song, the lark was borne,
In whirling spirals, tier on tier,
Far through the golden atmosphere.

Then sighed the Wandering Angel sore ;
    And turned one lingering look, and last,
Upon the dead : and, rising o'er
    The lake, the groves, the dell, he passed
On sailing pinions, broad and bright,
Along the footsteps of the night,
And down the pathway of the wind,
    Until he faded westward far,—
A Glory in the deep enshrined,
    The brother of the morning star—

And dropt upon the burning bar
Of the horizon, and passed on
Under its shadow, and was gone.

And loud and shrilly sang the lark ;
  And lovely waxed the risen day,
And laughed through every dewy spark
  That on the groves and meadows lay ;
And all the level leas o'erflowed
With light ; and all the copses glowed
Throughout ; and over every slope
Trembled a glory, like the hope
Of future summers, seen through tears
Of autumn, down the rolling years ;
And from the bosom of the brook
A thousand happy murmurs shook ;
And on the still and smiling lake,
The lingering lilies seemed to wake
Once more into their bygone bloom,
And breathed a soul of fresh perfume :
And all the sombre cypress lit
In the light shaking over it ;
And even the hoary willow took
A smile from Nature's happy look.

But softly round the cypress' foot
Hovered the shadows hushed and mute :
For there the mother and her child
Slumbered :—And still the mother smiled :
  For she had fall'n asleep in death,
  And yielded up life's troublous breath,
And in the Unknown found her child.

THE END.